SWAN LAKE

BY Nancy Ellison

RETOLD BY Amy Ephron

STARRING Nina Ananiashvili

Harry N. Abrams, Inc., Publishers

For Bill, my darling partner in life and art
and for Nina's Gregory

PREFACE

Swan Lake, the greatest ballet ever created, has accompanied me all my life. As a young child, I first heard Tchaikovsky's music for the second act. Instinctively, I knew this music should be danced to, not merely played in concert halls. *Swan Lake* was the first full-length ballet that I performed with the Bolshoi, barely a season after I became a member of the glorious company. The ballet was the first I danced outside of Russia, in 1982 in Hamburg, Germany. It was also the first one I performed in many other countries, including Japan, Sweden, Canada, Italy, and Yugoslavia, to name a few. And when I made my debut with the American Ballet Theatre— my other "home" company—I danced the role of the Swan Queen.

After all these performances, I am still in love with *Swan Lake.* And I believe that as long as a ballerina in the white costume of the Swan Queen stands backstage listening to the music of Tchaikovsky and preparing herself for the entrance of Odette, ballet will be alive and well.

— Nina Ananiashvili, 1999

Introduction

Five miniature palaces—by the edge of a lake—built for swans! My husband Bill and I were location scouting with Nina Ananiashvili and Gregory Vashadze and had arrived at Kuskovo Palace, our first stop—but there would be no other sites to visit! I was enchanted by the idea of swan palaces—where else to shoot Nina and the Bolshoi dancers in *Swan Lake*.

Kuskovo, just outside Moscow, had been the treasured family estate of the Counts Sheremetyevs, one of the most glorious names in Russian aristocracy since the fifteenth century.

The Grand Palace situated by the lake was completed in 1775. Designed in the classic style of the eighteenth century, the wooden palace was the center of Moscow's elite cultural scene. Its breathtakingly beautiful ballroom was often used for recitals. Anton Rubenstein, Peter Ilich Tchaikovsky's teacher, performed there, and we can assume Tchaikovsky as a young music student did so as well. I could not help but imagine Tchaikovsky, during his years in Moscow when he composed *Swan Lake*, walking the grounds and seeing both white and black swans, gliding gracefully in the lake, with their miniature nesting palaces behind them. What a delicious opportunity for us to replicate the story/ballet of *Swan Lake* in this setting.

The whole of Kuskovo is quite magical. Besides the Grand Palace with its lakes and miniature swan palaces, the grounds of the estate house enchanting examples of eighteenth-century architecture from other European countries as well: a Dutch town house, a Swiss chalet, an enchanting mint-green Italian villa, and an elegant French-style orangerie. These were all built to amuse Catherine the Great on her visits to Moscow. Many of these exquisite buildings appear in our story. Kuskovo became our stage. Its history and grandeur became our inspiration.

I used to feel that my initial urge to photograph came from my own sense of curiosity, for photography has always been, obviously, a keen way to focus on life. However, I think there is an even greater drive than the voyeuristic joy of observation: the near spiritual elation from holding the moment where the ephemeral or even the trivial becomes solid — monumental. Photography can freeze you in time and place, allowing one the lingering reality of a private world.

Photographing dancers is, for me, a collusion between the hunted and the hunter, seeking to achieve together one exact moment of creative perfection. Dancers, even as young students, are driven to meet an ideal of form and technique. Fingers, toes, mind, spirit must all come together. What extraordinary subjects! Notice for example Alexei Fadeyechev's hands, for they are always expressing the character or story line of a scene. Alexei retired soon after our shoot to become Artistic Director of the Bolshoi. Like his legendary father, Nikolai Fadeyechev, who partnered Prima Ballerina Galina Ulanova, Alexei had a brilliant career as Premier Danseur and as Nina's partner. How lucky we were that he performed for us! Nina Ananiashvili, arguably the finest Prima Ballerina dancing today, has not only flawless technique and style, but her mischievously scintillating spirit and energy was omni-present throughout the session. The fairy tale magic of Kuskovo Palace and its grounds enchanted Nina. She "nested" serenely into each location and was very much a part of the process. It was Nina's innate sense of the essential *Swan Lake* that I fell back on when faced with the challenge of attempting to visualize a fairy tale as a silent film captured in still photographs of dancers frozen in time set to unheard music!

Photographing *Swan Lake* presented me with two problems: The first was creating an ending that both satisfied our concept of the story and dealt with our physical limitations. Traditionally, after the evil sorcerer Rotbart tricks the Prince into betraying his love of Odette, the Prince is forgiven, Rotbart is vanquished, and Siegfried and Odette float off together in eternal bliss. We decided to leave Rotbart unharmed as the Prince realizes the horrific consequence of his actions. The lovers are reunited in eternal love by the symbolic still waters of our lake. The second obstacle we encountered was dealing with the time frame of our story, which traditionally takes place at night. Faced with *no* ambient lighting of any kind necessary to create an effect of night indoors in the ballroom, and faced with shooting *every* exterior image day-for-night, we all agreed to set the story in daylight, which violates the premise that the swans turn into beautiful maidens only at night. Amy Ephron, in her retelling of our tale, created the necessary variation to our story.

How lucky we were to have the gracious cooperation of the Kuskovo Estate administration and staff! To them and to Gregory, Nina, Alexei, Dmitri Rodionov, Tatiana Rastorgueva, the late Alexander Bogatyrev, and the members of the Bolshoi, I am deeply grateful.

— Nancy Ellison

SWAN LAKE

Once upon a time, a young Princess named Odette lived in a kingdom in Russia. When

she was barely nine, her parents died and she became the Queen. An evil sorcerer named Von Rotbart put a spell on

her, transforming her and her handmaidens into swans, and banished them from the Kingdom, so that he and his

daughter Odile could reign. But from the moment Von Rotbart ousted Odette, it was as if all light had left the king-

dom, and the land was shrouded in darkness, the Palace covered in ice.

Years later, in a Kingdom just to the south, there lived a Prince who was coming of age. Prince Siegfried's twenty-first

birthday was the following day. The Palace was alive with activity, acrobats and magicians

practiced their tricks in the courtyard, strains of Tchaikovsky symphonies wafted softly in from the Great Hall, and

the garden overflowed with lilies and wild roses. Prince Siegfried should have been excited at the thought of the

upcoming celebration but he was not. For his parents (the King and Queen) had demanded that he pick his bride

at the Grand Ball. And though no one had ever told him this sage advice, Prince Siegfried believed he should marry

for love. He was well-acquainted with all the beautiful and eligible young women from the Kingdom who had been

invited, and none of them possessed his heart!

THE PALACE GROUNDS

Despondent, morose, and full of longing, Prince Siegfried wandered into the Palace Gardens. He was struck by the appearance of a flock of white swans winging their way gracefully through the sky. Siegfried watched as they flew off so beautifully, almost in formation.

Prince Siegfried, lost in his own thoughts, soon found himself at Swan Lake.

The afternoon sun reflected across the waters of the still lake,

gray, glistening almost silver in the sun's rays. The Prince wasn't surprised

when the flock of swans landed on the surface of Swan Lake.

But when they dived below and then emerged, each one transforming

into **a beautiful young woman** dressed in a costume

of downy feathers, he was awestruck.

The leader was the most beautiful, elegant, and graceful of all.

Do swans have Queens?

he wondered.

She ran to him,
her feet barely
touching the ground.

They were shy with one another at first.

But he knew from the moment their eyes first me

at she might be his Queen.

Prince Siegfried took her in his arms and began to dar

He was afraid to even ask. Afraid that if he let her

th her. It took him a while to learn her story.

she might transform back into a swan . . . **and he would lose her.**

Finally, Queen Odette, for it was she;

did tell him her history,

explaining about the spell.

She also told him that Von Rotbart's magic was not all powerful—Odette and the handmaidens could transform into their human shapes either in the gardens along the banks of the lake or between the hours of midnight and dawn, at which time they could travel about freely. And if ever a Prince were to fall in love with Odette and keep his vow of faithfulness, the spell would be broken forever! As she was telling Prince Siegfried her story, the evil Von Rotbart was hiding nearby and overheard their every word. He saw the way they looked at one another and the way Prince Siegfried held her in his arms . . .

The sorcerer was furious—the reason why he had transformed Odette to a swan in the first place was that it had always been his wish that his own daughter Odile marry Prince Siegfried. Queen Odette was the only young, eligible woman in all of Russia who was more beautiful than his own daughter . . . and thus, Von Rotbart had always sworn to keep Odette and the Prince away from each other.

Von Rotbart saw that Prince Siegfried was enchanted with Odette and could not bear to let her from his arms. When he heard the Prince vow to love Odette forever and ask her to be his wife, Von Rotbart revealed himself to Odette, without Prince Siegfried seeing him. Odette was terrified.

Four of the youngest of the swanmaidens

(they were no more than cygnets), also unaware of the presence of Von Rotbart, began to dance and made a pretty little group of their own.

Allowing themselves to be distracted,

Odette and Siegfried watched the swanmaidens dance for a moment and then, oblivious

once again to everything around them, found themselves in each other's arms.

Prince Siegfried and Queen Odette made a sacred vow to each other that she would come
to the Grand Ball at the Palace the next night, just after midnight,

where he would publicly choose her as his bride and introduce her to the
Kingdom . . . and then, the spell would be broken forever!

Odette followed Siegfried through the gardens that edged the banks of the lake. She could not bear to part with him. When they reached the Palace, Prince Siegfried put his hand up to stop her. He was frightened that if she went further, she would be transformed back into a swan, and he might never see his **beloved Queen Odette again.**

THE GRAND BALL

The next day, at the Palace, everyone was surprised at Prince Siegfried's

change of mood. He was lighthearted and joyful, smiling the way

one does when he has found a certain love.

But he said nothing of it to anyone.

All over the Kingdom, beautiful young women were primping and preening,

lacing themselves into beautiful gowns and satin slippers, and

borrowing their mothers' finest jewels, each hoping that the

Prince would choose her as his bride.

Upon arrival at the Grand Ball, the princesses

and court ladies in attendance flirted shamelessly

with Prince Siegfried.

All of the women vied for his

attention, each hoping to be

selected as his royal bride.

None guessed that he had

already **promised his heart.**

But in the Kingdom in the North, in the Palace that was once the home of

Queen Odette, a different preparation had taken place. The sinister sorcerer Von Rotbart had dressed his own

daughter Odile for the Ball. By means of evil enchantment, by use of the darkest magic of its kind, he had trans-

formed his daughter Odile into the living image of Queen Odette. Odile, who was as wicked and deceitful as her

father, was determined to make Prince Siegfried her own. But since there was no light in the Kingdom any more,

every time Von Rotbart tried to create a gown for her that was as pure and white as Odette's, he had no success.

The dress, though a replica of the one Odette would wear, came out as black as night.

An hour before midnight, a woman no one in the kingdom had ever seen before

swept into the ballroom on the arm of a sinister-looking

man who was so well-dressed that his evilness could

be mistaken for elegance.

Although the woman was dressed in black,

the likeness was so

striking that Prince

Siegfried mistook

Odile for his own

Queen Odette.

SEDUC
S

He took her in his arm

…d began to dance with her. He did not think to check the time.

Odile, acting her part so beautifully, danced as the Swan Queen had danced with him the night before. Dancing

with him, dancing for him, displaying herself to everyone in the Kingdom. Prince Siegfried asked

Odile to be his bride and she accepted. He danced across the room to present her to the King and Queen.

As Prince Siegfried made his declaration

to his parents and, in error (such a fatal error it was), presented

them Odile, a crash of thunder was heard from outside.

Only then did Prince Siegfried have a vision of the frantic "white swan" Odette. He realized he had

been unfaithful to her, that he had been tricked by the evil sorcerer, and that the woman to whom

he had promised himself was not his beloved Odette. And now Odette and her handmaidens,

because of him, were condemned to remain swans forever . . . .

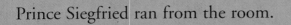
Prince Siegfried ran from the room.

Von Rotbart transformed

himself into an owl,

exposing himself as the evil bird of prey that he was,

and followed Siegfried from the Palace.

PREDATOR

THE PALACE GROUNDS

Prince Siegfried ran directly to the lake. Swan Lake.

He found Queen Odette weeping, surrounded by her mournful handmaidens.

"Believe me when I tell you that I didn't know," Prince Siegfried told her.

"Believe me when I tell you that it was you to whom

I thought I was promising myself.

I have never loved another. I will never love another."

AGONY

Odette forgave him instantly.

But the spell was stronger than either of them.

TOGETHER

Her heart had broken so completely that she felt herself

transforming back into a swan, and, in so doing, losing her hold on life.

She could not have borne the thought of living without him.

FOREVER

And, as Queen Odette felt her life slip away,

the evil Von Rotbart swept her up in his arms and held her triumphantly.

Prince Siegfried reached out his hand to her and in one last touch . . .

. . . followed her into the depths of the lake, where in a last embrace,

they were joined together in eternal love.

CAST

Odette, Odile	Nina Ananiashvili	(Prima Ballerina, The Bolshoi Ballet, American Ballet Theatre)
Siegfried	Alexei Fadeyechev	(Former Premier Danseur, currently Artistic Director, The Bolshoi Ballet)
Rotbart	Ilia Ryzhakov	(Soloist, The Bolshoi Ballet)
Hungarian Bride	Inna Petrova	(Ballerina, The Bolshoi Ballet)
Spanish Bride	Tatiana Rastorgueva	(Soloist, The Bolshoi Ballet)
Russian Bride	Irina Serenkova	(Artist, The Bolshoi Ballet)

CORPS DE BALLET

Julia Efimova, Anna Grishonkova, Elena Bukanova, Marina Zharkova, Olga Sokolova, Elena Neporozhnaya, Ludmila Ermakova, Svetlana Rudenko, Elena Dolgaleva, Tatiana Kurilkina, Olga Lipai, Nina Kaptsova, Olga Shtik, Marina Zakharova, Irina Serenkova, Irina Fedotova

CREW

Wardrobe	Natalia Zinovyeva
Make-up	Lydia Scherbakova, Alexander Shevchuk
First Camera Assistant	Nicholas Kuskin
Second Camera Assistant	Kenneth Ferdman
Photographer's Apprentice	Aviv Winer

LOCATION

Kuskovo Palace, Moscow, Russia

Editor: Howard W. Reeves
Designer: Roger Gorman

Library of Congress Cataloging-in-Publication Data

Ellison, Nancy,
     Swan lake / photographs by Nancy Ellison ; text by Amy Ephron
          p.   cm.
     Summary: Photographs and text present a retelling of the ballet in which an evil sorcerer
attempts to thwart Prince Siegfried's love for Princess Odette.
     ISBN 0-8109-4192-9
     1. Swan lake (Choreographic work)-Pictorial works-Juvenile literature. [1. Swan lake
(Choreographic work) 2. Ballet.] I. Ephron, Amy. II. Title.

   GV1790.S8 E44 2000

                                                  99-042147

Photographs copyright © 2000 Nancy Ellison
Text copyright © 2000 Amy Ephron
Published in 2000 by Harry N. Abrams, Incorporated, New York

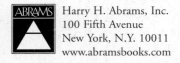
Harry H. Abrams, Inc.
100 Fifth Avenue
New York, N.Y. 10011
www.abramsbooks.com